This Little Tiger book
belongs to:

_____

_____

_____

This book is dedicated to anyone who has ever
owned a smelly, stained, muddy, sticky, painty,
VERY loved blanket ♥
- A M

To Erin, for endless support and helping me
to remember to eat at deadlines
- K A

**LITTLE TIGER PRESS LTD,**
an imprint of the Little Tiger Group
1 The Coda Centre, 189 Munster Road, London SW6 6AW
www.littletiger.co.uk

First published in Great Britain 2017
This edition published 2018
Text copyright © Angie Morgan 2017
Illustrations copyright © Kate Alizadeh 2017

Printed in China • LTP/1400/1805/0217

2 4 6 8 10 9 7 5 3 1

# That is actually MY blanket, Baby!

Angie Morgan • Kate Alizadeh

LITTLE TIGER

LONDON

Once upon a while ago, there was a
brand new baby called Bella,

who had a brand new blanket
called Blanket.

Bella **loved** Blanket.
Everywhere Bella went,
Blanket **HAD** to come too.

Together Bella and Blanket explored the world, and as Bella grew bigger and bigger . . .

she grew to love Blanket more and MORE.

Bella and Blanket did **everything** together like painting stuff,

and sticking things to other things,

and **singing** and **dancing** in muddy puddles.

SPLOSH!

Then one day, a brand new baby arrived who had a brand new blanket of his own.

Bella **loved** New Baby.
In fact, she loved him almost as much
as she loved Blanket.

But she thought she would love him
**even more** if . . .

. . . he didn't **cry** so much.
"Don't cry, Baby," said Bella.
But New Baby went on crying.

So Bella tried **tickling** him,

and New Baby **cried** —
**even
more.**

So Bella told him her very funniest joke,

but New Baby didn't laugh at all.

So Bella showed
him her favourite
**happy** dance . . .

. . . and New Baby **stopped** crying.

"That's actually MY blanket, Baby,"
said Bella. "You have a lovely
NEW blanket of your own."

But New Baby didn't want his
boring new blanket.
He wanted Bella's sparkly, muddy,
painty, smelly one.

"Oh dear," said Bella.
She wasn't at all sure what to do.

So she thought a bit and wondered if . . .

once upon a while ago, Blanket had
been all clean and new too.

So she said, "I know, Baby . . ."

"If you take
your clean NEW
blanket . . ."

everywhere you go . . ."

". . . I will show you how to do stuff like painting, and sticking things to other things, and singing and dancing in muddy puddles."

"And when you have grown
as big as me, Baby,
you will love your blanket
ALMOST as much . . ."

"... as I love you."

# More books to love and share from
## Little Tiger Press!

SQUISH SQUASH SQUEEZE!

Pop-up, pull-out ending!

Tracey Corderoy
Jane Chapman

There's a Bison BOUNCING on the Bed!

Paul Bright
Chris Chatterton

TINY TANTRUM

Caroline Crowe    Ella Okstad

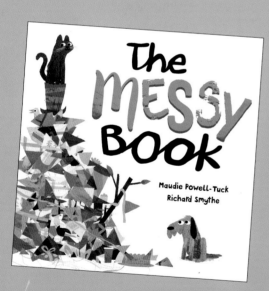

The MESSY BOOK

Maudie Powell-Tuck
Richard Smythe

FAIRY TALE PETS

TRACEY CORDEROY    JORGE MARTIN

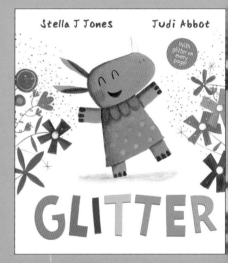

Stella J Jones    Judi Abbot

With glitter on every page!

GLITTER

For information regarding any of the above
titles or for our catalogue, please contact us:
Little Tiger Press, 1 The Coda Centre,
189 Munster Road, London SW6 6AW
Tel: 020 7385 6333
E-mail: contact@littletiger.co.uk
www.littletiger.co.uk